Herman
and the
Bears Again

Herman
and the
Bears Again

Story and pictures by BERNICE MYERS

SCHOLASTIC BOOK SERVICES

NEW YORK • TORONTO • LONDON • AUCKLAND • SYDNEY • TOKYO

To Craig

ISBN: 0-590-10243-5

Copyright © 1976 by Bernice Myers. All rights reserved. Published by Scholastic Book Services, a division of Scholastic Magazines, Inc.

12 11 10 9 8 7 6   3 4 5 6/8

Printed in the U.S.A.

Herman
was invited to
spend the week-end
in the forest
with his friends
the Bears.

He took the bus
to the last stop
and then
walked
the rest of the way
through the woods.

Little John Bear
was waiting for him
and together
they went
to the Bears' cave.

"He's here!"
called Little John.

"Hello, Herman.
How have you been?"
asked Papa Bear.

Herman
took some presents
from his bag
and gave one to
each Bear.

"Now let's all
go out and play,"
said Little John.

"Hide and seek.
Hide and seek!"

"Let's play
hide and seek."

"Herman's it!"

And while Herman counted,

all the Bears
ran
and hid.

A Scout Leader
saw Herman
and ran over to him.
"Don't cry,
you poor boy.
I'll take you home."

"Who's crying?"

"I don't think
your parents
would want you
to play
out here.
Don't you know
there are
BEARS
in the forest!"

"Sure
I know,"
said Herman.

"And bears
can be very dangerous."
The Scout Leader
took hold of
Herman's hand.
"You'll be much safer
back at camp
with us."

Near the first-aid tent
the boys
wrapped Herman
in a blanket
and gave him some soup.

"We'll take you home
tomorrow."

"I don't want to
go home.
I'm visiting
my friends and—"

But
Herman
never got to
finish
his sentence.

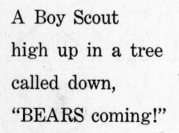

A Boy Scout
high up in a tree
called down,
"BEARS coming!"

The Scout Leader
began to shout
commands.

"Close camp.
Fold tents.
Fires out."

And they all
marched
to another clearing
in the woods.

"Where's Herman?"

No one knew.

"Let's go look for him,"
said the Scout Leader.

They found
Herman
standing in the middle
of their old camp
surrounded by
the bears.

"There he is,"
shouted the Scouts.
And they ran
toward him.

Quickly
they grabbed Herman
and ran back
the other way.

"He's safe now!"
they shouted.

"On to the camp, men!"

But where was
their camp?

"Maybe it's over there."

"I think we're lost,"
the Scout Leader said at last.

"Don't worry.
My friends
will find us,"
said Herman.

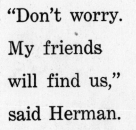

Just then
five very angry bears
appeared.

They had come
to rescue Herman
from the Scouts.

The Scout Leader
fell
to his knees.
"Please don't eat Herman.
Eat me.
Let the child live!"

The bears
just stared at him.

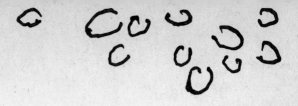

"My friends
don't want to eat anybody,"
said Herman.

"Friends?"
the Scout Leader said.
"These bears
are your friends?"

"That's what I've been
trying to tell you,"
Herman said.

The Leader
turned
to his troop.
"See,
there was
nothing
to be afraid of.
They're friends!"

Mama Bear smiled.
"Invite your friends
to have lunch with us, Herman."

"And after lunch
we'll all play hide and seek,"
said Little John Bear.

"Scout Leader's it!"

While he was counting,
a woman ran
up
to him.

"Don't cry.
I'll help you
find your way home."

"Who's crying?"

If you like this book,
you will want to read another
book about Herman and the bears —
NOT THIS BEAR!